D0365250

A Note to Parents and Caregivers:

Read-it! Readers are for children who are just starting on the amazing road to reading. These beautiful books support both the acquisition of reading skills and the love of books.

The PURPLE LEVEL presents basic topics and objects using high frequency words and simple language patterns.

The RED LEVEL presents familiar topics using common words and repeating sentence patterns.

The BLUE LEVEL presents new ideas using a larger vocabulary and varied sentence structure.

The YELLOW LEVEL presents more challenging ideas, a broad vocabulary, and wide variety in sentence structure.

The GREEN LEVEL presents more complex ideas, an extended vocabulary range, and expanded language structures.

The ORANGE LEVEL presents a wide range of ideas and concepts using challenging vocabulary and complex language structures.

When sharing a book with your child, read in short stretches, pausing often to talk about the pictures. Have your child turn the pages and point to the pictures and familiar words. And be sure to reread favorite stories or parts of stories.

There is no right or wrong way to share books with children. Find time to read with your child, and pass on the legacy of literacy.

Adria F. Klein, Ph.D.
Professor Emeritus
California State University
San Bernardino, California

Editor: Christianne Jones
Designer: Nathan Gassman
Creative Director: Keith Griffin
Editorial Director: Carol Jones
Managing Editor: Catherine Neitge
The illustrations in this book were prepared with acrylic paints.

Picture Window Books
5115 Excelsior Boulevard
Suite 232
Minneapolis, MN 55416
877-845-8392
www.picturewindowbooks.com

Printed in the United States of America.

Library of Congress Cataloging-in-Publication Data
Dahl, Michael.
Dust bunnies / by Michael Dahl ; illustrated by Hye Won Yi.
p. cm. — (Read-it! readers)
Summary: When "dust bunnies" grow under the bed, a child sweeps, mops, and dusts
in an effort to chase them away.
ISBN 1-4048-1168-0 (hard cover)
[1. Household dirt—Fiction. 2. Cleanliness—Fiction. 3. Stories in rhyme.] I. Yi, Hye
Won, 1979- ill. II. Title. III. Series.

PZ8.3.D136Du 2005
[E]—dc22
                                                          2005003739

Dust Bunnies

by Michael Dahl
illustrated by Hye Won Yi

Special thanks to our advisers for their expertise:

Adria F. Klein, Ph.D.
Professor Emeritus, California State University
San Bernardino, California

Susan Kesselring, M.A.
Literacy Educator
Rosemount–Apple Valley–Eagan (Minnesota) School District

PiCTURE WiNDOW BOOKS
Minneapolis, Minnesota

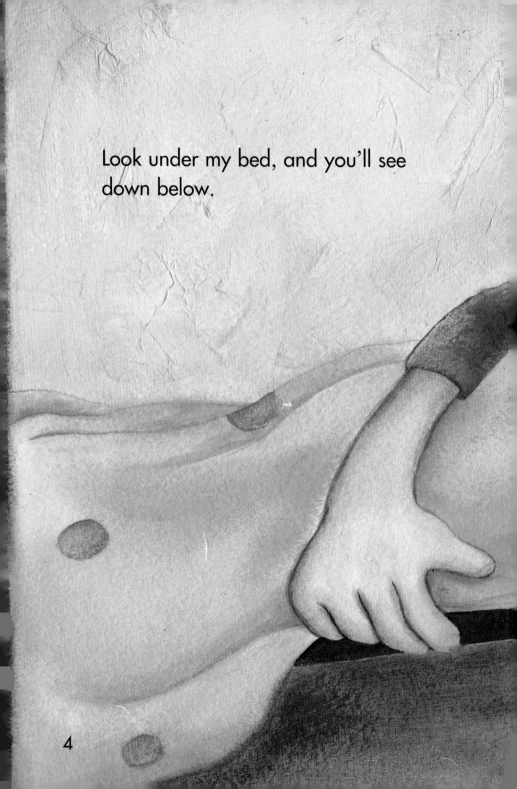

Look under my bed, and you'll see down below.

4

5

The one special spot
where the dust
bunnies grow.

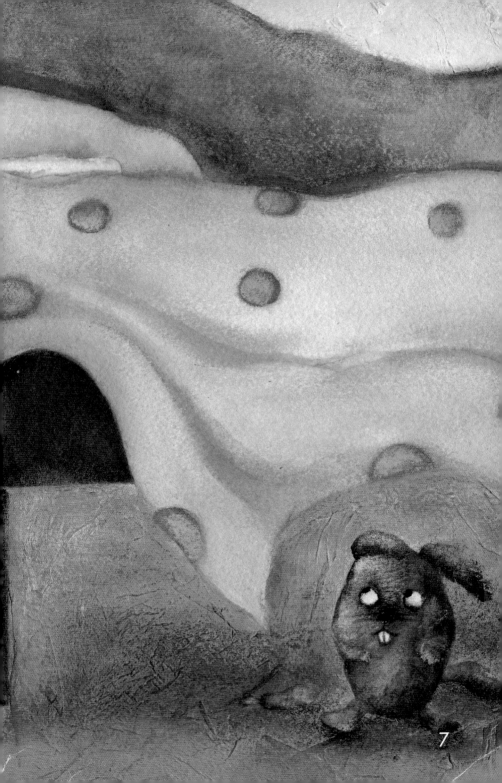

They feel safe down below where it's quiet and dark.

They don't make a sound.

They don't meow. They don't bark.

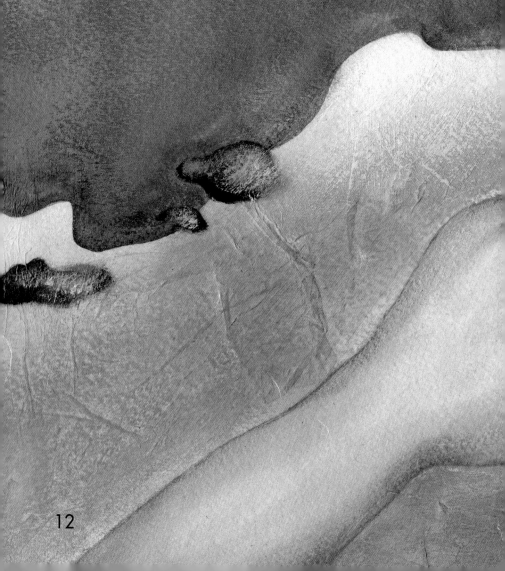

Dull pennies or buttons make
dust bunny eyes.

12

Their tails are small fuzz balls
or moldy French fries.

14

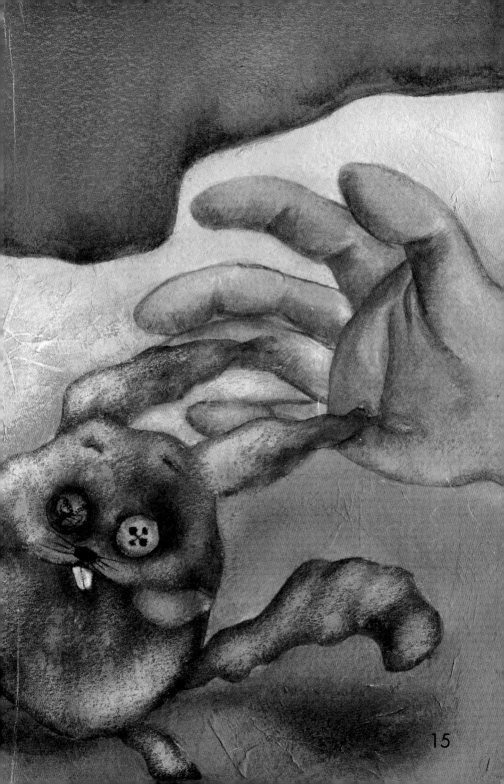

They don't eat a lot—just a crumb or a crust.

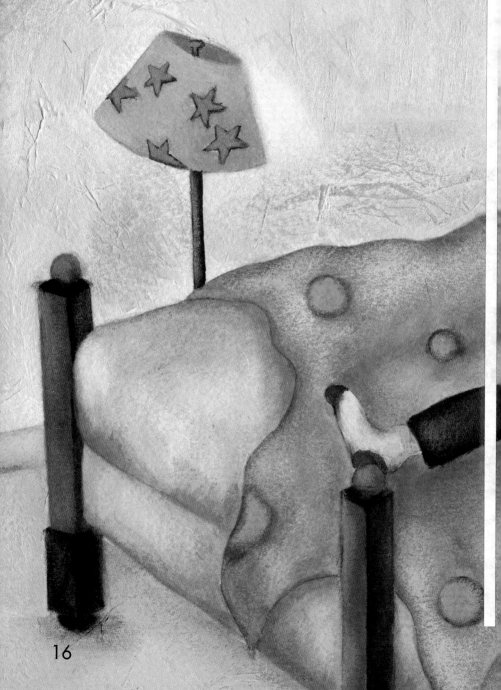

17

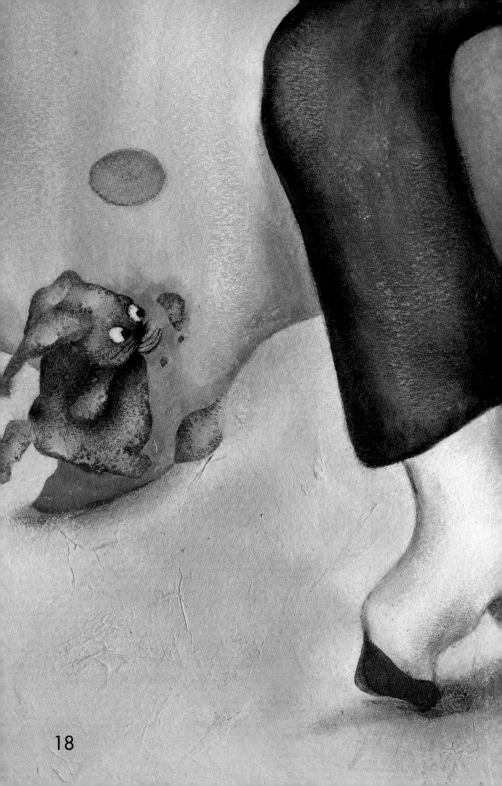

18

They lick up the lint, and they dine on the dust.

But one day, my mother was
helping me dress.

She yelled, "What a muddle!
This room is a mess!"

21

"You'll just have to sweep it, dust it, and mop.

When all the dirt's gone, then you can stop."

I washed and cleaned with
mop, bucket, and broom.

Until all of the dust bunnies ran
from the room.

I cleaned, and I cleaned.
It took quite a while.

I knew I could stop when
I saw my mom smile.

Now my room is all shiny, but wouldn't you know ...

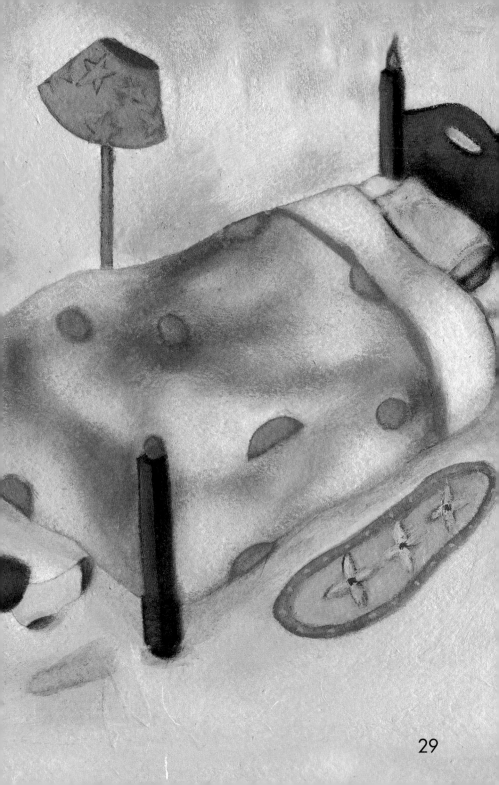

29

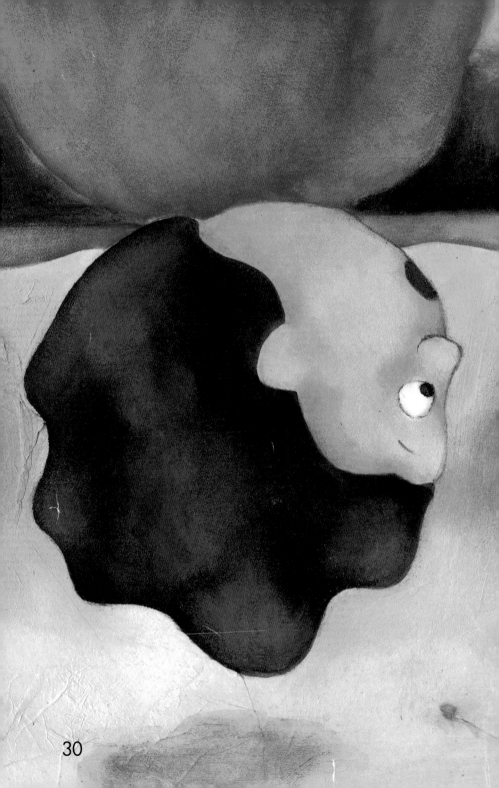

down under my bed, dust bunnies
still grow.

More Read-it! Readers

Bright pictures and fun stories help you practice your reading skills. Look for more books at your level.

At the Beach by Patricia M. Stockland
The Bossy Rooster by Margaret Nash
Frog Pajama Party by Michael Dahl
Jack's Party by Ann Bryant
The Playground Snake by Brian Moses
Recycled! by Jillian Powell
The Sassy Monkey by Anne Cassidy
What's Bugging Pamela? by Michael Dahl

Looking for a specific title or level? A complete list of *Read-it!* Readers is available on our Web site:
www.picturewindowbooks.com